FEAR

ISABELLE LYLE

To Cheline, Matthew, and Todd
Photographs by Donald Stickles

Reptiles courtesy of Arizona Sonora Desert Museum

Text copyright © 1989, 1974 by Isabelle Lyle.
Photographs copyright © 1989, 1974 by Scholastic Inc.
All rights reserved. Published by Scholastic Inc.
SPRINT and SPRINT BOOKS are trademarks of Scholastic Inc.
Printed in the U.S.A.
ISBN 0-590-35170-2

4 5 6 7 8 9 10   31   03 02 01 00 99 98

CHAPTER 1

It was a hot afternoon in Mexico. Rául sat inside a small school. He felt the sun as it came through the windows. It was warm.

Rául heard his teacher talking. But he was not really listening. He was thinking about what he had to do. And he was thinking that he could not do it.

His class was studying science. At the front of the room stood a table. There was an aquarium on the table. There were cages on it too. What Rául could not do was in the last cage.

Soon it would be his turn. He would have to go up to the table. He would have to put his hands into the cage. He would have to take it out. *A horned lizard!*

The teacher was going to talk about the lizard. Rául was supposed to hold it while the teacher talked. But Rául could not do that. He did not want to touch it. It was too ugly!

Rául knew that if he picked it up, he would drop it. Then everyone would know he was afraid.

From where he sat, Rául could see a caterpillar in the first cage. Rául wished he had to hold the caterpillar. It was small, and it had to be held on a piece of paper. But his friend Juan was going to hold it. It didn't seem fair. Juan was not afraid of the lizard. Juan was not afraid of anything.

Rául wondered if the teacher knew he was afraid. Did she want to make him show his fear to the class?

CHAPTER 2

The teacher was ready to start. Soon Rául would have to face the lizard. He tried to think of a way out, but he couldn't.

"This afternoon we will learn some new things," said the teacher. "Juan, will you come up here?"

Juan got out of his seat. He was smiling as he walked up to the teacher.

"Juan will show us the caterpillar."

I could do that, thought Rául. *Why did Juan get the caterpillar? Why not me? It's not fair!*

Juan opened the cage. He picked up the caterpillar and a bit of grass. Carefully he put

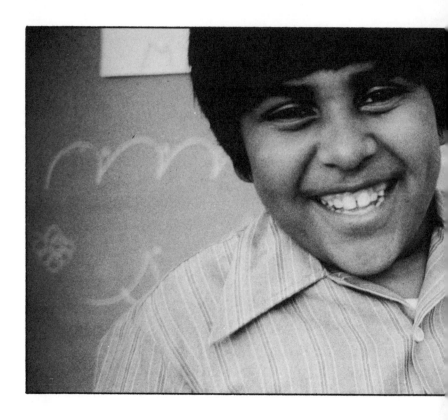

both on a piece of paper. The caterpillar was eating the grass. It did not move. *Oh, how easy,* thought Raúl.

"Soon the caterpillar will make a cocoon," said the teacher. "It will hide in the cocoon. And when it comes out, it will be a moth. That is fun to think about. It is like magic."

Raúl could think of something that would be real magic — a cocoon for him. A cocoon where he could hide from his fear.

Rita was next. She walked up to the aquarium. Raúl wondered if she was afraid. Tadpoles were a little ugly, and they were hard

to hold onto. Maybe she would drop it. If she did, her turn would take longer. But Raúl knew that would not help him. There would still be plenty of time for his turn.

Rita put her hand down in the water. She held up a tadpole. She was not afraid.

"Soon this tadpole will be a frog," said the teacher. "Its tail is getting short, and it is growing legs."

Rita showed the tail and the legs. No, she was not afraid.

Now it was Raúl's turn. The teacher turned and looked at him. Raúl wanted to hide.

CHAPTER 3

"Rául," said the teacher. "Will you come up and show the lizard?"

Rául did not move. He could not move. He kept thinking to himself, *Now everybody knows I am afraid.*

"Rául, what is the matter?" asked the teacher. Every eye was on Rául.

"Rául," said the teacher again.

But Rául could not answer. He could not do it. And he could not say he could not do it.

"I guess Rául is not feeling well today," said the teacher. "Will somebody else come up and show us the lizard?"

"I will," said Juan. And he jumped up and hurried to the cage.

Raul was ashamed. He could not look at his friend Juan.

"This is a horned lizard," said the teacher. "He looks very dangerous. But he only eats insects. Many people are afraid of him."

Again Raul felt all eyes looking at him.

"But the horned lizard is afraid of most things," said the teacher. "He does not fight."

Raul looked at the lizard. He wondered if the teacher had given him the lizard for a reason. Was the lizard like him?

The teacher told them, "The lizard is the same color as sand. And he lives in sand. When another animal goes after him, the lizard does not move. He stays so still it is hard to see him."

"But can he fight with his horns?" asked Rita.

"No," said the teacher. "The horns are just a trick. They make him look dangerous. But he is not.

"If another animal sees him, there is one more thing he can do. No one knows how he does it, but he can squirt red drops from his eyes."

"What for?" asked Juan.

"This makes him look hurt or dead. Then his enemies leave him alone. They think he would not be good food. But he can only do this when he is scared. *Very badly scared!*"

CHAPTER 4

School was almost over for the day. It was Friday. The caterpillar had to have food, and so did the lizard and the tadpole. It was a long time to Monday.

Juan wanted to feed the lizard. He knew where he could find a nest of ants. He asked Rául to help him. The two boys went outside.

"What happened before?" Juan asked. "You were going to show the lizard."

"I didn't feel good," said Rául.

Juan did not believe Rául, but he said no more about it. Rául was his best friend. He would not tease him.

Soon the boys had several big ants in a paper bag.

"Did you hear what the teacher said?" Rául asked. "The lizard makes blood come from his eyes!"

"Yes," said Juan.

The boys went in. Rául held the paper over the cage. He started to shake the paper. The ants dropped off.

But the shaking paper scared the lizard. It backed into a corner and tried to hide.

Rául liked making the lizard afraid of him.

All day the lizard had filled him with fear. Now it was his turn to fill the lizard with fear.

"I'll make it cry blood," said Rául. And he started to shake the paper some more.

The lizard had no place to hide. And soon the red drops came from its eyes.

Rául kept shaking the paper. He was shouting and laughing.

The lizard tried to climb up the side of the tank. Then it fell on its back and lay very still.

"Rául!" cried Juan. "Stop! It has almost stopped breathing."

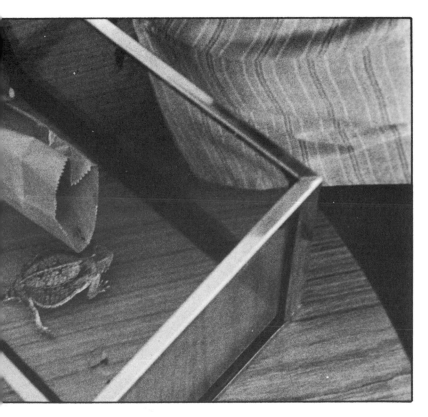

CHAPTER 5

Rául and Juan looked at the lizard. The teacher came over. She looked at it too.

"I am afraid he is very sick," she said.

"I was shaking the paper," said Rául. "I wanted to see him cry blood."

The teacher reached down and turned the lizard over. It was still breathing.

"I did not mean to hurt it," said Rául. He was trying hard not to cry.

"I know," said the teacher. "But the little lizard didn't know that."

"I'm sorry," said Rául. "I hope he'll be all right."

Then he and Juan picked up their books. They walked to the door.

"Boys, it may not be all your fault," said the teacher. "Remember, we found him by a road. He could have been hurt by a car."

"We'll come to school tomorrow," said Juan. "The janitor will be here. He can let us in. We'll feed the lizard some more ants. That will make him feel better. And this time we'll be very quiet."

Raúl smiled. "The lizard will get better when he finds out we're his friends."

The next day was Saturday. But Raúl went to school. He stopped at Juan's house.

"Look!" said Juan as he ran out of the house. "I have a piece of cardboard. It won't rattle. The lizard will not be afraid."

The boys reached the school. The janitor was cleaning the steps.

"Good morning," Raúl said. "We came to feed the lizard."

The janitor stopped his cleaning. "The lizard is dead. He was dead when I came this morning."

"It was my fault," said Raúl. The two boys walked away.

"The teacher said the lizard might have been hurt by a car," said Juan.

"But I made it worse," said Raúl. "I made it die of fear!"

CHAPTER 6

Rául couldn't stop thinking about the lizard. It had made him look like a coward in front of the whole class. So he had been glad to learn that the lizard was afraid. He had wanted to make the lizard feel as he had felt. But he hadn't wanted the lizard to die.

Now he was sorry for what he had done. And he knew what he must do now. He must find another horned lizard.

But horned lizards were special. And they were hard to find. Rául went looking. He looked along the road, in the fields, and down by the river. But he didn't find any.

There was one more place to look. He could go to Horse Head Ranch. He was sure he would find a horned lizard there. But that was not all he would find there. He would find rattlesnakes there too.

Rául was afraid again. He wasn't afraid of a horned lizard because now he knew it couldn't hurt him. But a rattlesnake was different! A rattlesnake could kill him with its bite.

Rául knew he would have to go to the ranch if he wanted a horned lizard. He also knew how dangerous it was. He thought it over and made up his mind. He would go in spite of the danger. But first he would learn about rattlesnakes.

That night at dinner Rául asked some questions of his father. "Papa," he asked, "what

do you do when you see a rattlesnake?"

His father laughed. "You stay away from it!"

"But what if you can't?" said Raúl. "What if it's in your way?"

"Kill him with a big rock."

"What if he strikes before you can hit him?" asked Raúl.

"He can't reach far unless he is coiled. If he is coiled, get some small rocks. Throw those rocks at him. That will make him unwind. Then he can't get you before you get him."

Raúl's father looked up from his dinner. "Why do you want to know so much about rattlesnakes?"

Raúl kept eating. He did not look up. "It is something for school," he said.

CHAPTER 7

The next morning Rául woke up thinking. He thought about the horned lizard. He thought about the long walk to Horse Head Ranch. And he thought about rattlesnakes.

Rául also thought about Juan. He wanted Juan to go with him. Surely the two of them could find a horned lizard. Also, Juan wasn't afraid of anything. If Juan was with him, Rául would not be so afraid.

He asked Juan to go.

"Not on your life!" Juan answered. "Horse Head Ranch is too far away. It's a crazy thing to do!"

"I've walked there before," said Rául. "It's not too far."

"You've walked there with your father," said Juan. "But not by yourself. Besides, think about the rattlesnakes! I wouldn't go there for anything!"

Rául was surprised that Juan would not go. Maybe Juan was not as brave as he had thought.

"Come on, Juan," Rául said. "We'll find another horned lizard. Besides, I know how to kill a rattlesnake. Papa taught me. I'll go with you, or I'll go without you!"

"Well," said Juan, "you're my friend. And I'm

afraid for you to go alone. I don't know how far I'll go. But I'll start out with you. Then we'll see."

After two hours of walking in the hot sun the boys were tired. "How much farther?" asked Juan.

"We must be halfway," Rául answered. "Let's rest."

They sat down on a big rock and looked around. There was nothing to see but sand and rocks.

"It's a long way to the nearest house," said Juan. "No one could hear us call for help."

"I could hear you. And you could hear me," Rául said. He was trying to sound braver than he felt.

The boys got up. They began walking again. They still had a long way to go.

"We were foolish to come," said Juan.

Rául didn't answer. He wanted to be quiet. He wanted to listen. He was sure he had heard something.

Then there was a loud crash. Something jumped in the air and ran in front of them.

Juan cried out. He started to run.

Rául screamed too. But he didn't run. Soon he began to laugh.

Juan came running back. "What was it?" he asked. "A wildcat?"

Rául laughed again. "If we're afraid of a rabbit, we're really in trouble!"

CHAPTER 8

Again Rául was surprised at Juan. Juan had run. Maybe Juan was more like him than he had thought. Or maybe he was more like Juan. Juan had never said he was not afraid of anything. Rául had just thought that. Rául had thought so much about his own fear. He had never thought that other people could be afraid too.

Both boys were now very tired and hot. They kept on walking, but Juan began to drop behind.

Then Rául heard it. It was a rattling noise. *Now I must show Juan*, Rául thought. *I said I knew how to kill a rattlesnake. First I must see the rattler. I must find out if it is coiled.*

He could tell where the noise was coming from. But he could not see a snake. There was only a small plant. It wasn't large enough to hide a snake. But Rául picked up a rock.

It was Juan's turn to laugh. "Are you going to kill a locoweed?"

Rául dropped the rock. He laughed too.

The boys stood there. They watched as the wind blew the locoweed. The seeds inside the weed rattled. The sound was like the buzz of a snake.

"Let's talk this over," said Juan. "Must we go

to Horse Head Ranch? It's dangerous, and we may not even find a horned lizard there."

"You don't have to go, Juan," said Rául. "But I do. I decided to go. I have to get another lizard!"

"I said I would start with you," Juan said. "I've done that. Now I'm going back. I wish you would come back with me. I'm afraid for you. You must be afraid too."

Rául smiled. "Yes, I am. But I must go."

Rául watched his friend walk away. *Yes, I am afraid,* Rául thought. *I'm like the little lizard. I, too, may die of fear!*

CHAPTER 9

Rául made it to the ranch. The first thing he did was rest. Then he heard the sound. He went stiff with fear. He wanted to run, but he couldn't move. He was afraid to move even his eyes.

It has really happened! he thought. *The snake will bite me, and I'll die. What shall I do?*

Then he remembered what his father had said. Kill him with a big rock. Yes, that was it. That was what he must do.

Rául make his legs stand up. He made them walk in a large circle. He had to find out where the sound was coming from. But he was afraid to look, so he kept his eyes closed.

He could hear the rattling sound. He wondered if that was how the paper had sounded to the lizard. And was he going to be like the lizard?

No! Not like the lizard! He opened his eyes. And there it was. A big rattler.

Rául looked at the snake. It was coiled and ready. He picked up some small rocks.

Rául's hand was shaking. He threw a rock. But it missed. The snake did not uncoil.

"Uncoil!" cried Rául. Then he threw another rock. This time he hit the snake.

It loosened a little. But it kept on rattling.

Rául threw two more rocks. Both of them hit the snake.

This time it straightened out. It began to move away.

Rául knew he had to move fast. The snake was getting away.

CHAPTER 10

Rául felt braver. The snake was trying to get away from him. He picked up a large rock and ran closer. He lifted the rock high. He was ready to throw it with all his strength.

Then he knew that the snake was filled with a great fear. He slowly let down his arms. He let the rock fall to the ground. He stood there and watched the snake crawl away.

He knew his own fear and the lizard's fear. He could understand the snake's fear.

Rául felt very tired. He was hot and lonely, and he wanted to go home. He decided he would not look for a horned lizard. He would give up.

As he walked along, he thought about how the snake could have killed him. That made him afraid again. He thought he heard rattling behind every bush.

Then something moved in front of him. Rául jumped over it and started to run. He ran until he fell down. Then he looked back. He could see what had scared him. It was a horned lizard. He ran back and picked it up.

Rául walked home, happy. He was almost singing. It would be hard to wait until Monday. Then he would take the horned lizard to school. Everybody would see he was not afraid of it.

Rául would make sure that no fear came to his new lizard.